MW00917050

THE NO-PHONE KID

LEONARDO LESAGE

Illustrated by Kylie McCoy

WISE LION
PRESS

Published by Wise Lion Press

Copyright © 2023 by Leonardo Q. Lesage

All rights reserved. No part of this book may be reproduced or transmitted in any form or by any means, electronic or mechanical, including photocopying, recording, or by any information storage and retrieval system, without permission in writing from the author, except for the inclusion of brief quotations in a review.

This is a work of fiction. Names, characters, businesses, places, events, and incidents are either the products of the author's imagination or used in a fictitious manner. Any resemblance to actual persons, living or dead, or actual events is purely coincidental.

ISBN-13: 979-8-3765-4513-3

Cover design by Ellen Meyer and Vicki Lesage
Cover illustration by Kylie McCoy

TABLE OF CONTENTS

CHAPTER 1: THE NO-PHONE KID

HERE AT OAK RIDGE MIDDLE SCHOOL, phones are more common than having hair on your head, but there's one person who doesn't have one, Tyler Tanner.

"Hey Tyler, check this out!" Kai shouted from across the hall at his locker.

"All right, but it better be quick because I have math in one minute," Tyler told Kai.

"Look at my new U-Phone 12," Kai said, breathing fast like he had just run a mile.

"Kai, why are you out of breath?" Tyler asked, concerned.

"I just had Spanish and I'm in a rush for science class, so see you later!"

Kai took off like a rocket down the hall. You could tell that he ran track. He was almost as fast as Usain Bolt and kinda looked like him too.

Tyler thought about Kai's new phone. Just last month, Kai had a U-Phone 10, and now he already had a newer model. It seemed like everyone in the whole school had a U-Phone. Except Tyler Tanner.

As Tyler headed to math class, his friend Jake, who was almost a year older than him but was a lot shorter, walked by.

"Meet you at the basketball court after school," Tyler said to Jake.

"Yep, see ya," Jake responded.

Jake was Tyler's best friend. Or maybe Kai was. Or maybe he had two best friends. Tyler had been friends with Jake since first grade at Clayworth Elementary. He and Kai had become friends last year when they were partners on a science project.

After school that warm March day, Tyler met Jake at the basketball court at Oak Ridge Middle School. There were enough hoops for lots of kids to shoot at the same time. It was a favorite place to hang out.

While Jake and Tyler were shooting baskets, Jake couldn't stop talking about his phone. Tyler felt left out because he only had a really old M-droid that didn't even work. He also was annoyed that everybody else got electronic gadgets for

Christmas and that was all they ever talked about even though Christmas was months ago. Why couldn't they just shoot hoops instead of talk about electronics *all the time*.

I need to get a phone, Tyler said in his head. *I don't want to be the only kid without one.* He was frustrated that his mom wouldn't get him one.

And he couldn't buy a phone himself because he had no money. He spent all his Christmas cash on NBA All-Star action figures and spent all his allowance on baseball cards.

Getting a phone was going to be like making a half-court shot at a basketball game—a giant challenge.

CHAPTER 2: TYLER'S FIRST IDEA

THAT NIGHT AT DINNER, Tyler brought up the subject with his parents.

"Can I get a new phone?" Tyler asked. He was stuffing some meat into his mouth.

"If you get a couple hundred bucks then sure," Mrs. Tanner said sarcastically.

"Please!" Tyler begged.

"Maybe when you're older," his dad said.

"Pleeeeease, all my friends have one."

"Well, maybe all your friends don't blow their money as soon as they get it," his mom said. "You should think about *saving* instead of *spending*."

Tyler went to his room and plopped on his bed. He dropped his head with a sigh and said, "I guess I'll be left out forever."

He emptied his piggy bank and started counting out his money. It didn't take long—he only had $10 from last week's allowance. He would have had $20, but he spent the previous week's allowance on a snack with Jake.

Now that I think about it, Tyler said to himself, *Mom does kind of have a point. I do spend my money as soon as I get it.*

But he couldn't help it! He liked doing things for his friends. It just meant that he never had any extra money.

As he lay in bed that night, Tyler thought about how he could get some money to buy a phone. He came up with his first idea and couldn't wait to wake up the next morning and get started. Then he could come up with more money-making ideas later. He figured he would need about $200. Maybe $250, to be safe.

LEONARDO LESAGE

Goal: $250

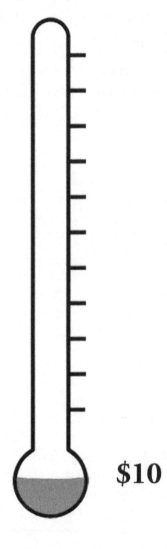

$10

CHAPTER 3: CAKE WALK

THE NEXT DAY WAS SATURDAY, and Tyler woke up at 4:00 AM to get ready for his two-day family vacation in Nashville, Tennessee.

He planned to find money on the ground because people drop money all the time in big cities. It would be a cake walk, even though he wasn't totally sure what that saying meant.

In Nashville, Tyler and his family did all sorts of interesting things. They visited the capitol building and the Country Music Hall of Fame. They walked all over the city, and his parents kept saying things like, "Look how neat that building is!" or "That house is so pretty, right Tyler?" But he wasn't really looking—his eyes were on the ground, searching for coins.

When they got home, Tyler added up all the money he collected: five pennies, three nickels, two dimes, and a quarter.

Tyler was mad. He felt like stealing a phone from the store, but he knew that was not the right thing to do.

On Monday, Tyler and Jake were talking about random things while shooting hoops after school. Tyler was happy that for once Jake wasn't talking about his phone. He didn't feel so left out, but he still wanted to get a phone for himself.

LEONARDO LESAGE

Goal: $250

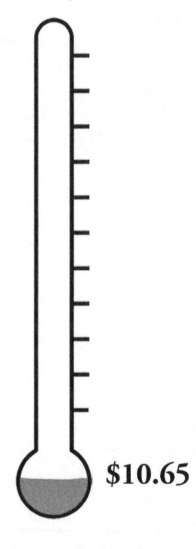

$10.65

CHAPTER 4: HARD WORK AND YARD WORK

AFTER COLLECTING ONLY 65 CENTS on the ground in Nashville, Tyler realized he needed to come up with better ideas to get more money.

"Aha!" Tyler shouted. "The most obvious way to get money is chores."

Tyler rushed to his mom.

"What is it, Ty?" his mom asked. "You're not usually that excited when you come home from school, especially on a Monday."

"Do you have any chores I can do?"

Mrs. Tanner was surprised because Tyler never wanted to do chores.

"Well, if you really want to, you can sweep the kitchen and dining room."

"Great!" Tyler said. "How much will you pay me for that?"

"Oh, *now* I understand why you want to do chores. Okay, I'll give you $1.50 for both rooms."

Tyler got right to work. After five minutes, he was already done. He asked his mom for another chore. But the chore Mrs. Tanner gave him was very challenging—folding four days' worth of laundry.

Four days! I'm gonna be rich after this, Tyler thought.

He told his mom, "Sure."

Then he folded and folded and folded. About 35 minutes later, but what seemed like hours, he was finally done.

"Hey Mom, I'm finished. How much money do I get?" Tyler asked.

"Well, that was a lot of laundry, so how about $1.10?" said Mrs. Tanner.

"WHAT! Only $1.10 for *that* much laundry?"

"Fine, how about $2.00?"

"Really? I knew I shouldn't have done chores for you if that is all I'm going to get," Tyler said with a grumpy voice. "I'm going to ask Sam if I can do chores for him."

Tyler went outside and saw his neighbor Sam sitting on his front porch chair reading the newspaper.

Tyler walked up to Sam and started talking to him, but Sam ignored him. Tyler got closer.

"HI, SAM!" he shouted. Now Sam looked up. He had trouble hearing sometimes.

"Oh, hi Tyler," Sam said slowly. He did everything slowly. He was pretty old.

"Can I do some chores for you?" Tyler asked.

"Why are you asking about a horse? I don't have a horse," said Sam.

"CHORES, not HORSE!" Tyler said loudly.

"Huh?"

"You know, CHORES, like making a bed or mowing the lawn," Tyler explained.

"Oh, *chores!*" Now Sam understood. "Why, yes, you can pull some weeds for me. I have tons of them in my yard."

After Tyler pulled every single weed, he went to Sam to tell him he was finished, but Sam wasn't on the porch anymore.

Tyler knocked on the door. Sam answered the door, looking confused.

"Hi, Tyler, what are you doing here?"

"I'm done pulling your weeds."

"Oh, that's right, I forgot. Let's see, I guess I should pay you something. How much do I owe you?"

Tyler thought about it for a minute. He didn't want to be greedy, but he had worked pretty hard.

"How about $15?" Tyler asked.

"Is that all? I think you deserve more than that. I'll give you $25."

A big smile appeared on Tyler's face. "Thank you very much, Sam."

LEONARDO LESAGE

Goal: $250

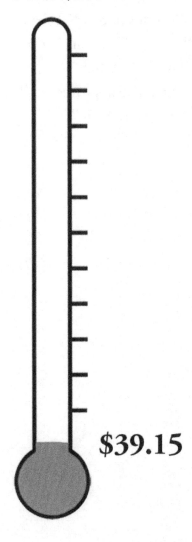

$39.15

CHAPTER 5: FRIENDSHIP BRACELETS

"TAYLOR, TIME FOR DINNER!" Tyler yelled to his little sister. They usually got along okay, but sometimes they fought. She was just a kid, only eight years old.

Taylor was making friendship bracelets. She had a whole pile of colorful bracelets: red, white, and blue; green, gold, and purple; and orange and black.

"I'm almost done making my bracelets," said Taylor. "I'll be there in a minute."

Tyler was about to head back to the kitchen when Taylor asked, "Wait, do you want one?"

"Sure." Then Tyler got an idea. Taylor didn't need all of those bracelets—she must have hundreds. If Tyler got some, he could sell them.

"Can I have more than one?"

Taylor handed Tyler four bracelets.

"Maybe a few more."

She gave him four more.

"Thanks, but how about a few more?"

Taylor asked, "Are you sure you need that many? How many friends do you think you have?"

"Well, the only friends *you* have are dolls!"

"Just for that, I'm only going to give you two more."

Tyler stuffed the bracelets in his pocket and ran down to dinner.

...

The next day at school, Tyler managed to sell all ten of the friendship bracelets but only earned a measly $5.

That was still a lot for him. Now his savings were up to $44.15.

Tyler wasn't going to give up. One way or another, he was going to get enough money for that phone!

LEONARDO LESAGE

Goal: $250

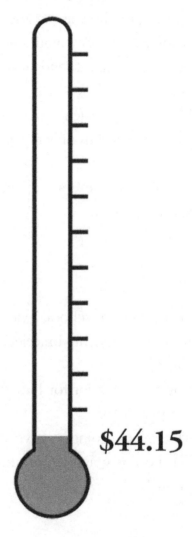

$44.15

CHAPTER 6: ROCKY, SPECKLES, AND SPOT

"WOOF, WOOF!" Tyler could hear Sam's dog, Rocky, who was a toy Australian shepherd, barking next door. Tyler loved dogs, although he didn't have one himself because his mom didn't think he was responsible enough to take care of it.

This gave Tyler an idea. He ran over to Sam's house.

"Hi, Sam, can I walk your dog for you?" he asked when Sam opened his door.

"What? You want to watch my hog?" Sam said.

"WALK YOUR DOG!" shouted Tyler.

"You mean Rocky?"

"Yes, ROCKY! Will you pay me to walk him

for you?"

"Sure," said Sam. "I'll give you $15."

Rocky flew out the door and started circling around Tyler and sniffing him. While Sam went inside to get the leash, Tyler picked up Rocky so the little dog wouldn't run away.

Sam came back with the leash and said, "Good luck!"

Tyler and Rocky started walking down the street. Rocky ran around in circles and Tyler had to keep untangling the leash.

As he walked past the Williams' house, Tyler saw Mrs. Williams with her two dogs, Speckles and Spot.

"Hi, Tyler, I see you're walking Rocky. Do you want to walk Speckles and Spot too?"

Speckles had long, curly fur with lots of dots and Spot was all white with one big spot on his back.

"Sure! How long do they need to walk?"

"About a half hour, if that's okay."

Tyler and the three dogs continued walking down Deer Meadows Lane.

When Tyler, Rocky, Speckles, and Spot were

at the end of the neighborhood, they headed toward the park. Suddenly Rocky spotted a squirrel. Then Rocky took off chasing it. Tyler couldn't hold on to the leash because Rocky was too fast.

"No, Rocky!" Tyler yelled. Then Speckles took off too, chasing Rocky.

Tyler raced after them when he realized he wasn't holding on to Spot anymore. Everybody at the park was staring at Tyler. Then a familiar face walked by.

"Hey Kai!" called Tyler. "Can you help me round up these dogs?"

Kai chased after Speckles while Tyler chased after Rocky. They managed to grab their leashes.

"Where's Spot?" asked Tyler.

They found Spot taking a nap on a bench.

"There you are, Spot," said Tyler.

He thanked Kai and continued his walk. "Bye, Kai!"

●●●

After Tyler returned the dogs to Mrs. Williams and Sam, he earned all together $45— $15 from Sam and $30 from Mrs. Williams. He put the cash in his piggy bank right away.

That is a lot of money but it still isn't enough for a phone like Jake's, Tyler thought.

"Mom, can I use your phone for a minute?"

"Sure," Mrs. Tanner yelled from the kitchen.

Tyler hurried to the kitchen and grabbed her phone.

He went onto Google and searched for ways

to earn money. He was scrolling down when he bumped into an ad saying, "Now hiring referees for soccer games."

He clicked on the ad and it asked for an email and phone number. "Mom, can you put in your email and phone number so I can be a ref?" Tyler asked.

"It's okay for you to be a referee, but only if you ref Taylor's games," she said. "Here, hand me my phone and I'll get you all set up."

LEONARDO LESAGE

Goal: $250

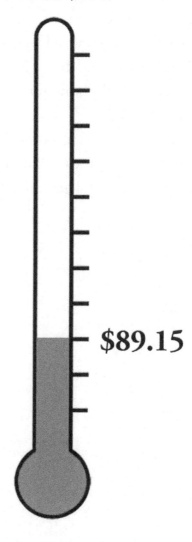

$89.15

CHAPTER 7: BUMPING UP THE CASH

IT WAS PITCH DARK, and Tyler Tanner could not fall asleep.

He thought back on his week. Wednesday had been Tyler's first time reffing, at one of Taylor's games. It was harder than he thought it would be. At some points, he couldn't tell if it was offsides or onsides. He was exhausted. He ran even more than the girls did. He also got tired of blowing the whistle every two seconds. But he earned $45!

Later in the week, he had refereed another game, and next week he would ref two more. That would be $180 to add to his savings!

KNOCK, KNOCK.

"Hello," Tyler's mom whispered from outside

the room.

"Hi, Mom," Tyler whispered back.

"It's 11:50. You better get to bed."

"I know, but I'm so excited," Tyler said in a loud whisper.

"About what?" his mom asked, walking into the room.

"Tomorrow Jake will help me find a new phone."

"Jake shouldn't have to pay for a phone for you."

"Don't worry, I'm paying for it myself."

"But I thought you only had $10 in your savings."

"I earned $250 from chores, dog-walking, and refereeing," Tyler said in a proud voice.

"That's a lot of money! Well, you better get some rest. Sounds like you have an exciting day tomorrow!"

• • •

VROOM, VROOM.

"The bus is here," Tyler said.

"Okay, honey, have a great day," Mrs. Tanner said.

"I will."

Tyler waved to his mom as he walked up the bus stairs.

"Hey, Tyler," Jake said. Jake lived two blocks away and got on the bus one stop before Tyler. Tyler sat down next to him.

"I'm ready to buy a phone," Tyler told Jake. "We can go today, right?"

"Are you sure you have enough money?" Jake asked.

"Yeah, I have $269.15 in my savings."

"Uh oh, that's not enough. Do you have any more?" Jake said.

"What do you mean? U-phones are about $250, right?"

"This one cost $900." Jake pulled out his phone from his pocket.

"Oh, come on! I worked so hard," Tyler whined. He was stressed.

Jake tried to cheer him up. "You don't really need a phone. I barely use mine, only to call and text people."

"Exactly! I want to be able to call and text you even when you're not around. I want to stay connected to my friends."

"I get it. I'll try to come up with some ideas so you can make more money."

Tyler felt a little bit better. But how would he get the rest of the money he needed?

●●●

DING, DING!

"Hi, class. Today we will be testing what we've learned about World War II," said Mrs. Sippi, the history teacher.

Tyler was so distracted about what Jake had said to him he forgot what he was supposed to do.

"I'll pass out the test and as soon as you get it you may start," Mrs. Sippi said.

Uh oh, thought Tyler. He took a deep breath, then started taking the test.

Before he knew it, Mrs. Sippi was talking. "Students, you may head to your next class," she said.

"Yay, P.E.!" P.E. was Tyler's favorite class. He was about to run out the door when Mrs. Sippi stopped him.

"Not so fast."

She grabbed Tyler's test and showed him his grade.

"You got a D-. I expect a lot more from you,

Tyler." She wrote "WORK ON" at the top of the paper.

"Sorry, I was distracted," Tyler said.

"Just make sure you focus next time."

"All right. See you tomorrow."

●●●

"What took you so long? P.E. started five minutes ago," Jake said.

"I don't know, but let's just go to the court."

Since the weather was warm enough, they were allowed to go outside and do whatever they wanted, as long as they were active. Tyler sprinted off faster than an Olympic track gold medalist.

"Wait up Tyler! I'm coming." It took a second for Jake to catch up.

"Tyler…" Jake started.

"Yeah?" Tyler responded. He knew Jake was gonna talk about his phone.

"I was thinking, what if we have a garage sale at my house? I have a lot of old toys we can sell," Jake suggested.

"But what do I do if it's your sale?" Tyler asked.

"Well, my dad will let you make signs and fliers, maybe some price tags."

"And maybe my mom will let me sell some of my own stuff!" Tyler said.

"Great! It will be in three weeks on Saturday morning."

"COOL, I AM SO EXCITED!"

Tyler was pumped. He was inching closer to getting that new phone. Then *finally* he wouldn't be the only kid in school without one.

New Goal: $900

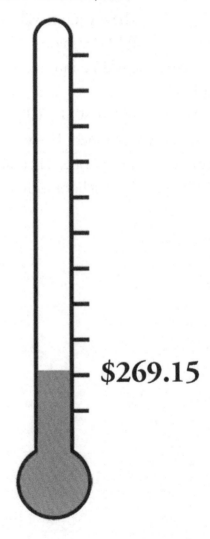

$269.15

CHAPTER 8: THE 12-YEAR-OLD

TYLER WOKE UP Saturday morning. Everything was quiet. Where was everybody?

He knocked on his parents' bedroom door, but no one answered and the room was empty. Then he went to Taylor's room to see if Mom and Dad were in there. But even Taylor wasn't there.

He decided to check downstairs. As he started down the stairs, he saw balloons. When he reached the bottom, his sister and his parents yelled, "Happy birthday!"

"Oh, it's my birthday?" Tyler asked. In all the excitement about earning money, Tyler almost forgot about his birthday. It was March 25. He realized he was now 12 years old.

Before he could even say thank you, he ran to the counter where he saw his favorite chocolate chip pancakes and a pile of presents. He knew it wasn't polite to open the presents right away. "Thank you, guys!"

He ate his breakfast quickly, then turned to the presents. "Not yet Ty, Taylor isn't done eating," his mom said. Tyler could tell Taylor was purposely taking a long time. He wanted to rip open his gifts before she was done, but he didn't want to be selfish on his birthday.

When she was finally finished, he started opening the presents. His mom had five uncles and seven aunts, and his dad had six uncles and six aunts. Most of the presents were cards from all of his great-aunts and great-uncles, with cash inside. Tyler opened the first card and saw it contained a letter and $10 in cash. The next one had $5. It didn't seem like much, but when Tyler added up all the money from all the cards, he had $180.

Mr. Tanner said, "There's one more present for you, Ty."

Tyler opened the last package. He found a signed baseball by his favorite player, Josh

Namber. Plus two $20 bills.

"Thank you, Mom and Dad!" Tyler was very excited about the signed baseball, but he was almost just as excited to get the money.

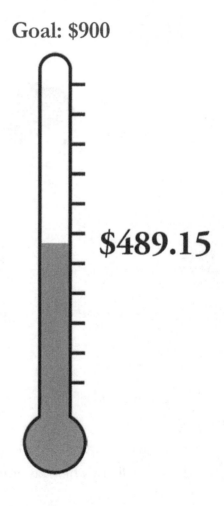

Goal: $900

$489.15

"I have so much money now," Tyler said. "I think I'll take a break."

He rode his bike over to Jake's house and they decided to go to Shake Ship and get milkshakes. Every time they went to Shake Ship, they got a pirate eye patch. They went to Kai's house and asked if he wanted to come too.

"I'll pay for it," Tyler said. He loved helping his friends out. That's why his money was always gone right away.

The shakes cost $5.79 each plus tax. The total came to almost $20.

When Tyler got home, he counted his money. He realized he now had $20 less to use for buying a phone.

This is why I never save any money, he thought. *I keep spending it on my friends. I'm not going to do it anymore. From now on, I'll just use my money for me.*

Goal: $900

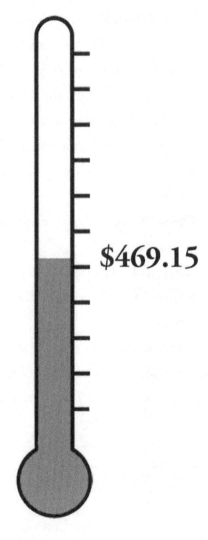

$469.15

CHAPTER 9: EASTERFEST

THE NEXT DAY, Tyler practiced his violin. He had been playing for two years and was getting pretty good at it.

Mrs. Tanner walked past his room and heard beautiful music.

"You sound really good, Tyler."

He put down his violin and smiled at her. "Thanks, Mom. By the way, it's time to pick up my new violin. I'll sound even better with that."

Mrs. Tanner and Tyler got in the car and drove to the local music store, Super Strings. After the store owner handed Tyler the new violin, he said, "Why don't you try it out?"

Tyler took the instrument and played his favorite song, Ode to Joy.

Ode to Joy

"Wow," the store owner said, "you sound amazing! Have you thought about auditioning for the fair?"

"You mean the Ballwin Easterfest?" Tyler asked.

"Yes. If you pass the audition, you join the orchestra and you can earn some money. You have a good chance of being chosen."

"That would be great," said Tyler. "I'm trying

to earn money to buy a phone."

"Well, you're selling that old violin, right?"

"Yeah, for $30," answered Tyler.

"I'll give you $50 for it."

"Deal!" shouted Tyler.

The next Saturday morning, Tyler headed to Blackhill Park for the audition with his new violin.

When he got there, he saw two people in front of him, a boy and a girl. The boy got on the stage and started playing. He sounded really good, maybe even better than Tyler. It made the butterflies in Tyler's stomach go crazy.

After the first person was done, it was the girl's turn. She was even better than the boy.

Then it was Tyler's turn. Tyler was super nervous, but he remembered that he had a new violin now and everyone told him how good he sounded. He gained his confidence, took a deep breath, and started playing.

After the audition, Tyler thought he did well and was relieved it was over. Now he just had to wait for the judge's decision.

●●●

"Tyler!" Mrs. Tanner called from the kitchen the next day. "I got an email about your audition."

Tyler raced into the kitchen. "Is it good news or bad news?" he asked.

"See for yourself," Mrs. Tanner said.

"No, you read it first! I'm too nervous." Tyler covered his eyes, but peeked out one eye to look at his parents.

"Dear Tyler," Mrs. Tanner read. "You did a wonderful job at your audition. Only 35% of auditioners got in. But you really stood out to us, and you are part of that 35%."

"Yippee!" Tyler shouted. "I'm in!"

"Congratulations, we knew you could do it!" said his dad.

"On April 8, please be at the park pavilion at 9:00 AM for the Ballwin Easterfest. You'll meet the rest of the orchestra and rehearse, then at 9:30 the performance will start at Stage B," Mrs. Tanner continued, reading from the email.

"I'm kind of nervous," Tyler interrupted. "I'll be on *stage*. In front of *people*."

"Can I finish reading, Tyler?" his mom asked.

"Oh yes, sorry," he said.

"After the performance, each member of the orchestra will receive a check for $80 and a gift card to Super Strings for $50."

"Well, that helps me be less nervous—that'll totally be worth it!" Tyler said. *Especially if I can exchange the gift card for cash*, he thought.

THE NO-PHONE KID

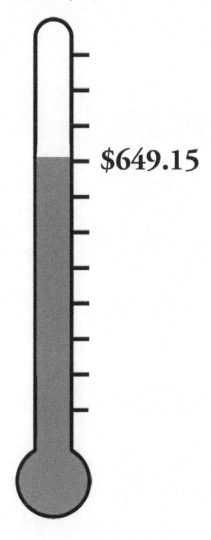

Goal: $900

$649.15

CHAPTER 10: THE GARAGE SALE

AFTER SCHOOL ON THURSDAY, Jake came over to Tyler's house and helped him gather up all his old toys, puzzles, hot wheels, and clothes that didn't fit him anymore to sell at the garage sale.

Tyler looked at his new NBA All-Star action figures. Should he sell them? He could probably get a lot of money for them, but they meant more to him than getting a little more saved for a phone. There were still plenty of other things he could sell.

Tyler looked at the pile.

"Jake, do you think this is enough stuff?" asked Tyler. "The garage sale will last all day and we might run out of things to sell."

"It's a lot, but probably not enough. You're right, we need more expensive items that people will pay a lot for," replied Jake.

"Well, my grandma has a lot of expensive junk in her basement. If she donates it, that would be big bucks for us."

Jake said, "Yeah, we should go over there. Will your mom take us?"

"Actually, my grandma lives down the street. It will just take a few minutes to walk there."

"Let's go!"

They ran out the door and down the street to Grandma's.

When they got to Grandma's house, she let them in and said it was okay to take some things from the basement.

"I never use that old stuff anyway."

In the basement, they picked out things they thought would sell. They found lamps, golf bags, a CD player and old CDs of musicals, Christmas ornaments and decorations, board games, an old clock, books, puzzles, and a foosball table that was in pretty good condition. But the thing Tyler and Jake were wondering about was a stuffed moose head. Who would want to buy *that?* But maybe someone would, so they packed it up with the rest of the stuff.

●●●

It was Friday night, the day before the sale. Tyler checked the neighborhood website.

"Mom, look! The website has every detail. Look, look, *look!*" Tyler was more enthusiastic than a person winning a billion dollars.

"That's awesome," his mom said. "Just remember, you have to get up early tomorrow morning so be sure to head up to bed soon."

●●●

"Hey Tyler, can you get the dinosaur action figures from that bucket?" Jake asked.

"Sure, should I grab the ninjas too?"

"If you want to you can."

Tyler and Jake were getting ready for the

garage sale. They only had one hour until people were gonna show up.

"Guys, it's time for breakfast!" Jake's dad shouted. STOMP, STOMP, STOMP.

Jake and Tyler came running down the stairs. The sale started at 7:30 AM so they needed to eat beforehand.

The first customer arrived, then another. There were more than 70 people. The big sale was going great.

•••

"That was a long day. We managed to get a lot of money." Tyler was excited.

"Let's count it up and see if it's enough for a phone," Jake said.

"One hundred, two hundred, three hundred, four hundred, five hundred…"

"$996!" Tyler shouted. "If we split it, my share is… $498!"

"If you add that to what you already saved, that's *more* than enough money for a phone!" Jake yelled.

With the extra money, he could buy the autographed Josh Namber baseball card to go with the autographed baseball he got for his birthday.

"Let's celebrate and get some dinner, boys," Jake's dad said.

LEONARDO LESAGE

Goal: $900

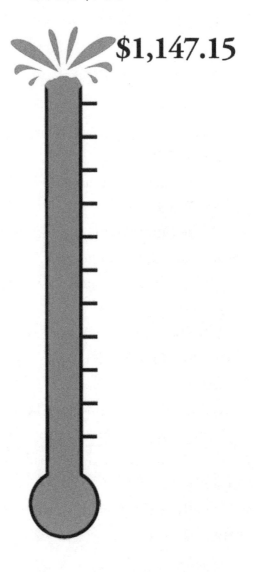

$1,147.15

CHAPTER 11: THE NOT-SURE KID

THIRTY MINUTES LATER, Tyler and Jake were eating some chicken at Blackhill Park.

"That chicken was finger lickin' good," Tyler said to Jake. "And this day was awesome! We got to spend the whole day together." *And we also didn't spend all of our time on phones*, he said to himself.

"Yeah, it was fun," Jake said, as he pulled out his phone. "I'm just gonna check something real quick, then are you ready to go to the store?"

"Sure," replied Tyler. *So much for no phones*, he thought.

"Wow, look at all the phones!" Tyler said. His jaw dropped.

Jake picked up a U-Phone 14. He handed it to Tyler and said, "This is one of the best phones you can get. It has a cool feature where you can ask the phone AI to message someone automatically. Here, try it out."

Tyler took the phone and played around with it.

"Isn't it so cool?" Jake asked.

"Yeah, totally," said Tyler. He sounded like he didn't really mean it. The phone he always thought he wanted didn't feel that special.

A salesman walked over to the boys. "Is that the phone you want?" he asked. "Sorry, we don't have any right now. But I can put your name on the waiting list. It should arrive in less than a week."

"Okay," said Tyler.

"I should warn you that you need to put down $25 to keep your place on the list," said the salesman. "That money is not refundable if you change your mind."

"Okay," said Tyler again.

•••

Ding! Mrs. Tanner's phone pinged with a message.

"Tyler, I just got a text from the phone store. Your phone is in. Ready to go get it?"

Tyler looked out the window as they drove to the phone store. He thought he would feel excited since he was finally getting his phone! But instead his stomach was in knots.

"Here you are," said the salesman, handing Tyler the new U-Phone 14.

Tyler took the phone and started to dig his money out of his pockets.

All of a sudden Tyler realized he didn't want to do this.

"Wait, I'm not sure I want to buy this anymore."

"Really?" asked Mrs. Tanner. "You already

put $25 down."

"If you don't buy this phone, you'll lose that money," the salesman reminded him. "I'll let you think about it for one more day."

Tyler was all mixed up. *I worked so hard to save for a phone, but I don't really even want one*, he thought. *My old beat-up phone is just fine. Why did I do all that work anyway?*

On the way home, Tyler realized that the reason he wanted a phone in the first place was to stay connected to his friends. And, well, because everyone else had one. Suddenly he knew that the best way to stay connected with his friends was to be with them in person, not on a device or screen. So... he could buy a basketball hoop with all that money! That way Jake and Kai could come over and hang out with him any time, without having to bike all the way over to the school.

"Stop the car!" Tyler shouted.

His mom pulled the car over into a parking lot.

"Tyler! What's going on?" she asked.

"I just realized that I want to buy a basketball hoop with my savings instead of a phone. It's better than a phone because you can stay connected in person instead of virtually."

"Are you sure? You worked so hard for that phone. And you'll lose your deposit."

"I'm sure. I know this is the best way to spend my money."

Tyler and Mrs. Tanner went directly to Tom's Sporting Goods where they found the perfect basketball hoop for $500. Because he had extra money, Tyler decided to buy two extra basketballs. That way, Jake and Kai could shoot hoops with him at the same time. Altogether Tyler spent about $575, including sales tax. He still had more than $500 left of his savings, even after losing the $25 deposit.

A big smile spread across Tyler's face. He was happy that now he'd be able to shoot hoops with his friends any time he wanted.

•••

"Hand me the screwdriver," said Mr. Tanner.

Tyler and his dad were setting up the basketball hoop in their driveway.

"Tyler!" Jake yelled as he pulled up in the driveway on his bike. "I think I left my phone at the park last night!"

Jake was really worried. The phone was super expensive. It was too late to go back because the park rangers cleaned up and picked up everything they found at 7:00 PM each evening.

"I can't buy a new one because my parents said they already spent too much money for my last phone. What am I going to do? I only have $700 in my savings and the phone will cost $900. I really need a phone!"

Jake stopped talking when he saw Tyler and his dad working on the hoop.

"What are you guys doing?" he asked.

"I chose to spend my money on a basketball hoop instead of a phone," Tyler said. "To me, it's better to shoot hoops anytime we want rather than calling or texting on a phone."

"Well, I kind of agree, but a phone is really important to me," said Jake. "What am I going to do?"

"I have about $500 left over. I can give you

$200 to help you get a new phone," Tyler suggested.

Even though Tyler really wanted to spend his remaining money on the autographed baseball card and keep the rest in savings for whatever came up next, he didn't like to see Jake unhappy. And now that he knew how to earn and save money, he would just have to wait to get that card. Being a good friend to Jake was more important.

After school the next day, Tyler looked back on how he thought he wanted a phone, worked and saved up for it, and then ended up buying the hoop instead. He felt pretty good about it.

I'm going to save the money I have left after helping Jake and keep on saving for other things, he thought. *From now on, if I want something, I'm not going to spend my money on useless stuff.*

Then he added, *Except when I want to treat my*

friends. They're important, too.

Jake and Kai came out of the school building.

"Hey, guys! Want to go to Shake Ship?"

"Sure, but this time, *I'm* paying!" said Jake.

The boys hopped on their bikes and raced as fast as they could to the Shake Ship.

A NOTE FROM THE AUTHOR

Hi,

It's me, Leo. Thanks for reading *The No-Phone Kid*. It was fun to write it and actually get it published!

I hope you liked my book. If you did, my mom says it would be really nice if you wrote a review on Amazon.com. I think it helps other people find it so they can read it too.

Thanks,
Leonardo Lesage

ABOUT THE AUTHOR

Leonardo Lesage was born in Paris, France and now lives in St Louis, Missouri with his mom, dad, and energetic sister. Leo attends elementary school, where he loves writing and also enjoys science and math. He has written many short books at school such as *World War 3*, *Soccer Stars*, and *Animal Battles*, but *The No-Phone Kid* is his first published book.

When he's not in school or writing, he enjoys playing soccer, shooting hoops, and running track. He also likes coding and playing video games and hanging out with his friends.

THANK-YOUS

I want to thank my mom, Vicki Lesage, and my grandma, Ellen Meyer, for helping me edit and publish my book.

And thanks to Kylie for doing the illustrations—it was so great to see my story come to life!

I also want to thank my fourth-grade teacher, Shannan Griesman, for supporting my story idea and for helping me become a better writer.

Made in the USA
Coppell, TX
16 October 2024

38714139R00049